For Lola

Weekly Reader Children's Book Club presents

Alexander

AND THE MAGIC MOUSE

STORY BY

MARTHA SANDERS

PICTURES BY

PHILIPPE FIX

AMERICAN HERITAGE PRESS
NEW YORK

There was once an Old Lady who lived in a house on top of a hill. It was the only hill for miles around. At the foot of the hill was the river and on the other side of the river there was

the town. After that, as far as the eye could see, there was only the great empty prairie.

The Old Lady was never lonely, for she lived with her animal friends:

a Brindle London Squatting Cat,

a Magical Mouse,

an Alligator from China, and a Yak. You may think

that is a strange household, but they got on very well together.

It is true that the Brindle London Squatting Cat, when he was not squatting in the sun on the doorstep, spent a great deal of time thinking about how to catch the Magical Mouse; but the Magical Mouse just made herself invisible and never got caught. Each day the Old Lady put out Magical Mousefood for the Magical Mouse, and each day the Brindle London Squatting Cat got ready to catch her. But the Magical Mouse had been invisible for so long that the Brindle London Squatting Cat had really forgotten what to look for, and he always fell fast asleep in his hiding place.

Alexander, the Alligator, had a mirror which the Old Lady had given him, and he liked to walk back and forth slowly in front of it, so as to admire his smile. His smile was almost three feet long; it took quite a while to admire it enough.

On warm days Alexander would waddle down the hill to the river and go for a swim near a sign the Old Lady had put up. It said BEWARE THE DANGEROUS ALLIGATOR. That was to keep people away. Alexander was not dangerous at all, but the Old Lady did not want him to frighten anyone. There are many people who cannot tell the difference between an alligator who is smiling and an alligator who is not smiling. But Alexander always hoped that if he smiled enough, people would understand how much he liked them. Sometimes when he was swimming he would poke his head above the water and

smile beautifully, in case anyone should be near. But the few people he saw always cried "Help!" and ran away. That made Alexander very sad.

As for the Yak, she was a lady Yak and gave each day a quart and a half of Yak milk, which was very rich and sweet and could be made into Yak butter and Yak cream. (As everyone knows, the Tibetans always put a little Yak butter in their tea to improve the flavor.) The Yak romped in the orchard and galloped up and down the hill. In summer she always brought the Old Lady a lovely fly swatter which she had braided from the long hairs of her tail.

And the Magical Mouse? She came with the house. She had always been there.

The animals all loved the Old Lady dearly. In her youth, the Old Lady, who was then a Young Lady, had been a great traveler. She went to many far lands. From each of her favorite places she wanted to bring something home. Not just a souvenir, but something really beautiful and interesting. So she asked the Brindle London Squatting Cat if he would come from England, and the Alligator if he would come from China, and the Yak if she would come from Tibet. And so the friends all lived together, along with the Magical Mouse.

Each afternoon at five the Old Lady rang a small shiny bell: tea was served. All the animals came into the drawing room and sat down and had tea and cakes and told what had happened that day.

The Brindle London Squatting Cat had to promise not to try to catch the Magical Mouse during teatime. All the same, the Magical Mouse made herself invisible. She never took chances. The Old Lady would put a bit of cake on the table, near the knitting basket, and presently it would be gone. Sometimes, as the cake was disappearing, the Brindle London Squatting Cat would forget himself and raise his paw over the place; then the Old Lady would look at him disapprovingly and say, "Now, now," and he would put his paw down again, frowning.

One fine afternoon in May, as they had all just sat down to tea and the Old Lady was about to ask them to tell their adventures, a tiny voice came from the knitting basket. Everyone was very surprised, for the Magical Mouse was shy, and never spoke unless she had something very important to say. They

waited in silence. Then the Magical Mouse squeaked, "It is going to rain for thirty days and thirty nights! My tail tells me so, and my tail is never wrong. We must get ready!"

The Old Lady got up and went to the window. There was not a cloud in the sky. "Are you sure?" she asked.

"My tail tells me so, and my tail is never wrong," said the Magical Mouse, and that was all she would say. Her feelings were hurt. She refused to tell when the storm would begin.

"Let us think," said the Old Lady, sitting down again. "We must have plenty of wood to burn, and plenty to eat, and a great many books and games to amuse ourselves with."

Then they all bustled about. The Alligator brought in logs of wood from the woodpile. The Yak dug up a supply of vegetables from the garden. The Old Lady looked in all the cupboards to be sure there was plenty of flour and molasses and marmalade and strawberry jam and pickled watermelon and

ginger tea. Everyone worked very hard except the Brindle London Squatting Cat, who finished his cake and went to sleep.

That night they went to bed feeling snug and safe and rather excited. They had gotten ready just in time, for very early the next morning it began to rain gently. By lunchtime the drops were coming down hard and fast. They built a cheerful fire and the Old Lady read sea stories out loud. It was like a holiday. From time to time they looked out the window at the gray rain falling and falling. What a splendid storm! They felt adventurous themselves, as if the house were a tall old ship that they were bravely keeping afloat.

But in the middle of the night the Old Lady suddenly got up and lighted a candle and went downstairs to the drawing room. "Magical Mouse, Magical Mouse!" she whispered. From between the sofa cushions came a sleepy squeak. "Magical Mouse, do you suppose they know, down in the town, that it's going to rain for thirty days and thirty nights? Surely the river will flood over its banks and wash the town away, unless the people try to stop it!"

"Nobody knows but us," said the Magical Mouse and that was all she would say. A tiny snore came from between the sofa cushions. The Old Lady shook her head in a worried way as she tiptoed back up the stairs.

"We must warn the people in the town," the Old Lady said at breakfast the next day, "for surely if it rains for thirty days and thirty nights the river will flood over its banks and wash the town away." Quickly she put on her knitted snood and her red flannel leggings with brass buttons and her black rubber galoshes. She got out her imitation fur muff and her umbrella

and went out the door. But soon she was back. "Too slippery," the Old Lady said.

"You could write a note," said the Yak, "and I'll go. I can run down the hill in any weather."

"Yes, yes, a note to the Mayor," said the Old Lady. She wrote:

> Dear Mr. Mayor:
> I am very sorry to tell you that it is going to rain for thirty days and thirty nights. Surely the river will flood over its banks and wash the town away unless you can think how to stop it.
> Sincerely yours,
> The Old Lady on Top of the Hill

The Yak took the note in her teeth and trotted out the door.
But soon she was back. "The bridge is washed out," said the
Yak, "and I can't cross the river."

"Then *I'll* go," said Alexander, "for I can swim *any* river."

"Be very careful, Alexander," said the Old Lady. She put
the letter in his mouth and off he went.

He slid down the muddy hill on his stomach, right into the
river. He began to swim, holding his head up high so the letter
would not get wet. The river was twice as wide as it usually
was and the water was dirty and cold. Alexander swam as hard

as he could, but the river was terribly strong. He swam and swam and *swam*. He thought he was going to be washed away completely. He puffed and panted and snorted. At last he reached the other side and crawled up the bank.

But where was the town? Alexander had been washed right past it! Now he had to walk back. It was a long way, and it is not easy for an alligator to walk even a short way. He trudged along, shivering and tired from his hard swim. Finally he saw Main Street ahead.

A man with an umbrella was hurrying down the street through the rain. Alexander went up to him, smiling, to ask where the Mayor lived. But the man dropped his umbrella, and ran down the street shouting, "Help! Help!" Alexander

shook his head sadly. Then he saw a lady. He smiled at her, even more beautifully. But she gave a scream and ran inside a store for safety. Then everyone on the street saw Alexander. They all yelled and screamed and dropped their umbrellas and ran away shouting, "Help! Help!"

Alexander was left all alone. He was ready to cry. He sat down on the empty sidewalk and tears rolled down both his cheeks, though they didn't show in the rain.

Soon a little boy came splashing along, enjoying the puddles. Alexander smiled sadly at him through his tears. The little boy stopped.

He said, "Hello! What's the matter?"

"Hello," said Alexander. "I've got to find someone who'll give an important message to the Mayor. Do you know where he lives?"

"Yes, everyone does, he lives at the end of this street," said the little boy.

"Would you give him this letter?" Alexander asked, opening his mouth very wide.

"Sure," said the little boy, reaching in and pulling out the envelope.

"Oh, thank you so much!" said Alexander. "Don't forget!"

"I won't, good-bye!" cried the little boy, and he ran down the street toward the Mayor's house.

Meanwhile, in the house on top of the hill, the Old Lady walked up and down, up and down. Night had fallen and still Alexander had not come back. "Where can he be?" The animals all were silent.

"I'm hungry," grumbled the Brindle London Squatting Cat, at last. "Let's have dinner!" The house seemed very gloomy. After dinner the Yak and the Cat played checkers in front of the fire. The Old Lady kept going to the door and looking out into the rainy night. Finally it was bedtime. It was very gloomy indeed.

The Old Lady could not sleep. In the middle of the night she got up and lighted a candle and went downstairs to the drawing room. "Magical Mouse, Magical Mouse!" she whispered. A tiny squeak came from inside the piano. "Magical Mouse, is Alexander safe?" The Old Lady's voice trembled.

"I think so," said the Magical Mouse sleepily, and that was all she would say.

The next morning the rain was pouring down as usual. The Old Lady went up to the topmost tower of the house and looked out with her telescope. At first she could see nothing but rain. Then she thought she saw people down by the river. They were building something — a wall made of bags of sand! So the Mayor had received her letter! But where in the world was Alexander? All morning she looked through the telescope, hoping to see him. The Brindle London Squatting Cat had to come up the winding stairs to remind her it was lunchtime.

In the afternoon the Old Lady went back to the tower. Now she saw a frightful thing: the sandbag wall was higher, but the river was higher, too. Which would win, the wall or the river?

By five o'clock it was too dark to see any more. She was just

about to ring the small shiny bell for tea, when the Old Lady thought she heard a sound at the door. It was a wet, scratching sound. She rushed to the door and flung it open. There was Alexander!

He was muddy and cold and tired and hungry. He had no sooner come inside than he began to sneeze. "Quickly! A towel and some hot ginger tea!" cried the Old Lady. They dried him off and gave him the tea and some supper and put him to bed. But he kept on sneezing. No one would say so, but everyone was very worried. Alexander was sick.

The next morning, before anyone else was awake, the Old Lady tiptoed up to the topmost tower to see if the wall by the river was still there. As she looked through the telescope she saw a huge wave coming down the river from far away. The

flood! It came nearer and nearer. But the townspeople had made the wall thick and high. The Old Lady held her breath. The wave came to the wall. The wave almost covered the wall. It almost went right over the top—but not quite! "Hoorray!" cried the Old Lady as the wave went on down the river. The town would be safe! She went to tell Alexander the good news.

But Alexander did not answer. He did not even smile. The Old Lady felt his forehead. It was very hot. "Oh dear!" she said.

"Oh dear, oh dear!" whispered the Cat and the Yak, who had come in to see how Alexander was. The Old Lady made

more ginger tea. The Yak made Yak butter especially to put
in it. Even the Brindle London Squatting Cat did his part: he
lay on Alexander's bed to keep his tail extra warm. But the
Magical Mouse could not be found.

That night, long after everyone else was asleep, the Old

Lady sat sadly beside Alexander's bed, ready in case he should want anything. At last she got up and went downstairs. "Magical Mouse, Magical Mouse, where *are* you?" she whispered.

"Asleep!" came a squeak from the chandelier.

"But Magical Mouse, how can I help Alexander?"

"Look on the tea table," said the Magical Mouse. There lay

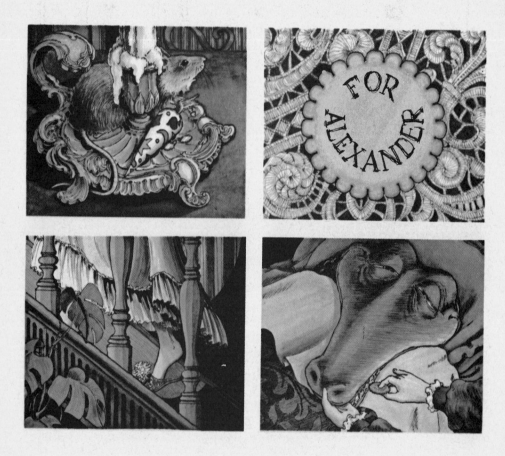

a tiny white cake. On it was written, in pink sugar letters, "FOR ALEXANDER."

"Oh, *thank* you, Magical Mouse!" whispered the Old Lady, and she tiptoed upstairs again. Gently she opened Alexander's mouth and put the tiny cake inside. As he swallowed he smiled, dreaming it was teatime.

The next morning it was as rainy as ever, but Alexander felt much better. After breakfast he and the Brindle London Squatting Cat played Monopoly on the bed until the Cat got cross because he was losing. The Old Lady was up in the topmost tower watching the river and the wall through the telescope. The town looked safe and secure.

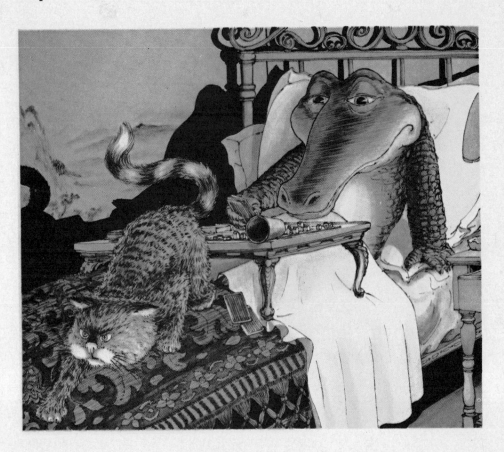

Every day it rained and rained and rained. They lost track of how many days it had been raining. They were out of pickled watermelon and molasses and they were tired of all their games and books. The Brindle London Squatting Cat was grumpy all the time. Even the Magical Mouse got bored and ate a hole in the knitting basket.

One day when she woke up the Old Lady had a funny feeling. What could it be? Something was different. The whole world was very quiet. Then she knew: the rain had stopped! The Old Lady jumped out of bed, and as fast as she could, she put on her knitted snood, her red flannel leggings with brass buttons, and her black rubber galoshes. She did not even stop to get her artificial fur muff.

"Lovely!" she said, looking at the bright sunshine sparkling on the wet leaves and grasses. Soon she was joined by all the animals. How glad they were to be outdoors again!

It was not long before the river had shrunk to its usual size. The townspeople took away the bags of sand and began building a new bridge. Soon the great rain and the flood were almost forgotten.

One warm summer afternoon the music of a brass band came floating in the windows. "My, my!" said the Yak, who loved music. They all ran to the front door to see what was happening. When they opened it there was the Mayor, just about to knock!

The band struck up a rousing tune. When it was done, the Mayor held up his hand for silence so he could make a speech. "Dear Madame, you were not forgotten," he said to the Old Lady. "On behalf of all the people of the town, with our heartfelt thanks, I wish to present you with this silver medal." And he reached into his pocket and pulled out a handsome red box which he handed to the Old Lady.

The band began to play again.

"Oh, no, it's not for me, it's for Alexander!" said the Old Lady. When the Mayor saw the Alligator he coughed nervously, but the Old Lady opened the box, took out the beautiful medal, and hung it proudly around Alexander's neck. She told the Mayor about Alexander's heroic swim. The Mayor and Alexander smiled shyly at each other. The Mayor even patted Alexander's nose. The band cheered.

Then the Old Lady invited everyone into the drawing room for tea. When finally all their guests had gone, the Old Lady and the animals looked at each other.

"My, *my!*" said the Yak.

"It is a *lovely* medal!" said the Old Lady.

"Humph!" said the Brindle London Squatting Cat, jealously, and he went off to take a nap.

Alexander just looked in the mirror and smiled. A tear of joy ran down his cheek. Inside a ball of yarn in the knitting basket the Magical Mouse smiled, too.

THE END